TED.

Book 6

The Rev Patrick Ashe is a retired vicar
who has worked for many years for the
cause of children, having been a chap-
lain for youth and the founder of two
relief organisations: Project Vietnam
Orphans and Christian Outreach. He
has seven children who were the first
to hear these stories before they were
written down for a wider audience.

By the same author:

Teddy Brown and the Aeroplane

PAT ASHE

KINGSWAY PUBLICATIONS
EASTBOURNE

Text illustrations and cover design by John Dillow

British Library Cataloguing in Publication Data

Ashe, Pat
  Teddy Brown and the aeroplane.
  I. Title   II. Series
  823'.914 [J]

  ISBN 0-86065-783-3

Printed in Great Britain for
KINGSWAY PUBLICATIONS LTD
1 St Anne's Road, Eastbourne, E Sussex BN21 3UN by
Stanley L. Hunt (Printers) Ltd, Rushden, Northants.
Typeset by Nuprint Ltd, Harpenden, Herts AL5 4SE.

For Robert
and all the children who listen
to these stories

Contents

A WORD TO
PARENTS AND TEACHERS

In the stories in this sixth book about Teddy
Brown, we learn that even sincere Christians have
'falls', but that God still loves them and wants
them to receive his forgiveness. Also that giving
can be fun, and that Jesus makes us more lovable.

At the end of the book there are suggested Bible
readings if you should want to get children used to
handling a Bible. I recommend using a modern
translation such as J. B. Phillips or *The Living
Bible*.

TEDDY BROWN
GETS UPSET

Even though Teddy Brown had asked Jesus to give him a new nature, his old nature was still there as well. Sometimes when we push Jesus out of the centre of our lives, we fall back into our old ways. This is what happened to Teddy Brown.

It was going to be Dutch Doll's birthday, so Robby said they could have a tea party. Dutch Doll was very excited, and there was a lot of chat among the other toys about where they were going to sit. Teddy Brown did not bother, as he knew he would be right up near the top of the table. But when he got to the party, he found that all the best seats had been taken. Dutch Doll had been telling everyone where to sit.

Of course Robby was at the head, because he owned all the toys. Dutch Doll was at his side, and then came her special friends, Toy Soldier, Mr Woollyhead, Elephant, Black-and-white Tiger, and then, towards the bottom of the table, Mona the Sad Dog, Pink Rabbit, Golden-haired Doll, and, right at the bottom, a place for Teddy Brown.

When Teddy Brown saw that he was at the bottom of the table, he was not at all pleased. He scowled. 'I'm not sitting there,' he said to himself, and he went off under the piano and sulked.

Under the piano was one of his 'prisons'— 'prison pride' Robby called it—and Teddy Brown's pride was very badly hurt. Robby went

and found him. 'What's the matter, Teddy Brown?'

'To think,' he said bitterly, 'that Dutch Doll should put me at the bottom of the table! She knows very well where I ought to sit. I ought to be on your left in a position of honour. I'm the most intelligent of all the toys, and I'm your best friend. I have always been friendly and helpful to her. It's a shame to treat me like this. I'm not going to the party at all. I shall sit here.'

'Oh dear,' said Robby, 'You're in a proper prison. Pride stops one doing all sorts of nice things. Its bars are worse than iron.'

'I'm not in prison,' said Teddy Brown, 'I can do exactly what I want.'

Robby smiled at Teddy Brown, and then he said, 'You want the best seat at the party, don't you? I'm going to tell you a story about a man who went to a wedding. When he got there, he had a look round at the other guests, and he thought to himself, "I'm the most important person here. I'll go and sit next to the bridegroom." So he went and sat down.

'A few minutes later the Best Man came up behind his chair, and said, "I say, old man, I'm awfully sorry, but this is Mr X's seat. Do you mind moving down?"

'So he shoved down one.

'A couple of minutes later the Best Man came

11

back, "Sorry, old boy, but Mr Y has arrived, and he is a very old friend of the bridegroom's. Do you mind moving down?"

'So he shoved down one more.

'A few minutes later the Best Man came up again. "Mrs Doodah is the bride's great aunt, and she would like her to sit here. Do you mind moving down?"

'So he shoved down another one.

'The Best Man came to him again. "Excuse me, but the next four seats are for the bridegroom's old school friends. Do you mind moving down?"

'Bounce, bounce, bounce, bounce—four times.

'All the other guests began nudging each other and smiling, and the poor man did not look at all happy. He thought he was the most important person, but the others did not seem to agree. He felt squashed.

'Do you know what he should have done?'

'What?' said Teddy Brown sulkily.

'He would have done better to go and sit at the bottom, and then the Best Man would have noticed him and said, "Won't you come and sit by the bridegroom's father?"'

Then Robby got out his *Living Bible* and said, 'Teddy Brown, you listen to this, because that was a story Jesus told.' And this is what he read: 'When Jesus noticed that all who came to the

12

dinner were trying to sit near the head of the table, he gave them this advice: "If you are invited to a wedding feast, don't always head for the best seat. For if someone more respected than you turns up, the host will bring him over to where you are sitting and say, 'Let this man sit here instead.' And you, embarrassed, will have to take whatever seat is left at the foot of the table.

' "Do this instead—start at the foot; and when your host sees you he will come and say, 'Friend, we have a better place than this for you.' Thus you will be honoured in front of all the other guests. For everyone who tries to honour himself shall be humbled; and he who humbles himself shall be honoured." '

When Robby had finished reading, Teddy Brown was very quiet. Then he said, 'You mean I shouldn't mind?'

'Yes,' said Robby.

'But I do mind,' said Teddy Brown.

'But you wouldn't mind if you let Jesus really rule your heart. Jesus did not stick out for the best seat in heaven. He was willing to give up everything and become a man, and then even let them crucify him.'

Teddy Brown realised that he had been pushing Jesus out of the centre of his life. Robby and he had a prayer together, and Teddy Brown asked Jesus to come back into his heart. He felt sweet inside again, and did not mind being at the bottom of the table, because Jesus was with him, and they all had a lovely happy birthday party.

So if ever you get upset like Teddy Brown, don't forget to ask Jesus to come back and be at the centre of your life, and he will take away all the hurt.

TO PODGE
WITH LOVE

Toy Soldier and his wife had a little boy called
Twirp. His ears were rather large, and his teeth
stuck out a bit, and he was very thin. Podge was
Golden-haired Doll's little boy. He was rather
plump, and sometimes looked goofy.

Just before Christmas their mothers had a ter-
rible quarrel. They had really got over-tired with
all the Christmas preparations—the cooking, the
shopping and the presents. Anyway, they had a
blazing row.

Now Podge and Twirp did not know that Jesus
said, 'It is more blessed to give than to receive.' In
fact, 'bless' and 'bliss' used to be the same word,
so that really means you get more happiness from
giving than receiving.

After the row, Golden-haired Doll and Mrs

Toy Soldier would not speak to each other. But they talked a lot to other people about each other, and their two little boys listened, and soon they also began to quarrel. They shouted rude things at each other like:

'Your Mum dyes her hair.'

'Your Dad beats your Mum.'

And a lot of other things that were not true at all.

They used to go and have fights behind the toy cupboard. Then suddenly, after about a year, their mothers made up their quarrel, and were ever so friendly.

But the boys were not.

Then Golden-haired Doll's little boy had a birthday, so Mrs Toy Soldier called her little boy and said, 'Listen, Twirp. It's your little friend Podge's birthday tomorrow.'

Twirp glowered. 'So what?' he said.

'You've got to give him a birthday present. How much money have you saved up?'

As there was no reply, she said, 'You must have nearly £3, so go and buy something for about £2. And mind it's something nice. Go on, do as I say!'

So he went and bought a Dinky Car, all in chrome and gold, with windows and sprung wheels and an engine and luggage at the back. It cost £1.99.

'That will do,' she said. 'And leave the price on.

They might as well know what we spent, then they might give you something nice on your birthday.'

Then she made him write on a card: 'To dear Podge, wishing you a happy birthday. Love from Twirp.'

And poor Twirp nearly choked.

He took it round, left it on the doorstep, rang the bell, and ran away.

Teddy Brown found him sobbing. 'What's the matter, Twirp?' he said.

'I've had to give that horrible Podge a birthday present—and I was saving up for some skates.'

After he had cried a bit on Teddy Brown's shoulder, Teddy Brown said, 'You know, Twirp, giving things can be fun.'

'Well I think it's horrible,' he moaned.

'Robby seems to love giving things away. Let's go and ask him why he likes it.'

So they went and found Robby, and asked him.

'You see,' said Robby, 'It's since I asked Jesus into my heart. Then I found I wanted to do what he said.'

'What did he say?' asked Twirp rather doubtfully.

Robby went and got his Bible, and found where Jesus said, 'When you do a kindness to someone, do it secretly—don't tell your left hand what your right hand is doing.'

17

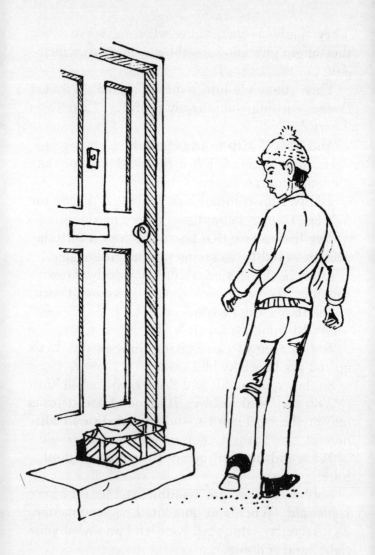

'Secretly!' Twirp looked amazed. Then he went on, 'Do you mean no name on it—no price ticket? I don't think Mum knows about that. She told me to leave the tab on so that they would know what it cost, and then they might give me something nice on my birthday.'

Robby said, 'What you give should be a secret between you and Jesus.' He got a pencil and wrote on a piece of paper,

'SECRETLY.'

Teddy Brown said, 'I got a present the other day, and I didn't know who gave it to me, so I was nice to everybody in case they were the one.'

'It's fun to have a secret just between you and Jesus,' Robby said.

'I like to give things to people I love,' said Teddy Brown.

'Oh yes,' said Twirp. 'It's all right giving things to your best friend. But not to someone like Podge!'

While they were talking, Robby had been turning over the pages of his Bible. 'Dad showed me this,' he said, and read out: 'Each one should give...not with regret or out of a sense of duty; for God loves the one who gives cheerfully.'

Twirp looked away. 'I didn't do that when I gave Podge his birthday present. I had to give it, and I hated giving it, and I wasn't a bit cheerful.'

Robby wrote another word on the paper:

'CHEERFULLY.'

Then Robby found something else Jesus said, and he read out: 'If you do good only to those who do good to you, why should you receive a blessing? Even sinners do that! And if you lend only to those from whom you hope to get it back, why should you receive a blessing? Even sinners lend to sinners, to get back the same amount! No! Love your enemies and do good to them; lend and expect nothing back.'

So Robby wrote on the paper:

'EXPECTING NOTHING BACK.'

Twirp was looking so horrified that it made Teddy Brown and Robby laugh. 'It's all right, Twirp. When Jesus is in your heart, you want to give like that, because Jesus gave everything for us. He gave his life and died on the cross. So you see, if we have his Spirit in our hearts, then we want to give too.'

Twirp took the piece of paper from Robby and looked at it for a long time. Then he asked him to write two words above, so that it looked like this:

'CHRISTIANS GIVE
SECRETLY
CHEERFULLY
EXPECTING NOTHING BACK.'

Twirp pinned the piece of paper up over his bed. And every morning and every evening he looked at it. The more he thought about it, the more impossible he knew it would be. He just hadn't got the right spirit.

One day Twirp said to Teddy Brown, 'It's all very well for Robby to write those words and for me to look at them—but I can't. When it's people I don't like, I know I can't give secretly, nor cheerfully, nor expecting nothing back.'

Teddy Brown knew how he felt, because he had been like that once. So he told him that he had been just the same, but how Jesus had given him a new spirit when he asked for it.

So they knelt down, and Twirp asked Jesus to give him his Spirit. A wonderful change came over him, and although he had his ups and downs, he discovered that with Jesus, he really enjoyed giving secretly, cheerfully, and expecting nothing back.

3

THE DREAM

Robby went to stay with a friend of his called Jemma for a few days, and he took Teddy Brown with him. Jemma owned a very beautiful doll with lovely fair hair that fell in waves down to her shoulders. She had bright blue eyes with long lashes. Her name was 'Beauty', and everyone who saw her said, 'Isn't she beautiful!' She really was lovely to look at.

But she was horrid! She was stuck-up and selfish and would not do anything for the little girl who owned her. If she did not get her own way, she used to lie on the floor and scream or go off into a sulk.

No one could call Teddy Brown handsome, but he was kind and thoughtful and always willing to do things for people and never minded if they did not say, 'Thank you.'

Teddy Brown's first meeting with Beauty was not very successful. Jemma had prepared a tea party, but Beauty said, 'I hate tea parties, they are so boring.'

'But Beauty, we have some visitors. Come and meet Teddy Brown.'

All she said was, 'I don't want to meet that ugly little bear—and anyway he looks stupid.'

Teddy Brown smiled at her, and tried not to be upset.

That night, Beauty had a dream.

She was in the garden with Teddy Brown, when suddenly she saw a little silver aeroplane coming down from the sky. A man got out. 'Would you like to go for a ride in my aeroplane?' he said. Beauty was just going to say, 'No, thank you,' when Teddy Brown said, 'Oh, yes please, we'd love to.' And he took her hand and pulled her into the plane.

Then, in her dream, Beauty felt the plane go up, up into the sky, right above the clouds. The plane stopped, and the pilot said, 'Have a look round, and then I'll take you back.'

So she and Teddy Brown set off together. As they went, she heard people saying, 'What a fine-looking Teddy Bear. Isn't he handsome!'

But she also heard the things people were saying about her. 'Poor little thing—isn't she hideous, with her ugly face and twisted legs. And she looks so sour and bad-tempered.'

Beauty was shocked. She had never heard that said about her. She could not believe her ears, so she went up to an old gentleman sitting on a bench.

'Please Sir,' she said. 'I wonder if you could explain something to us. Everybody always says I'm beautiful, but here they all keep saying I'm ugly.'

The old man said, 'Well, you see, here we see people as they really are, and when we look at you, we see that you are selfish, and that makes you ugly.'

'What about Teddy Brown?' she asked.

'Ah, Teddy Brown is sweet and kind, and we can see the loving spirit in his heart.'

When she woke up, Beauty remembered the dream very clearly, and it worried her, so she told Teddy Brown about it. She said, 'I had a queer dream last night, and an old gentleman told me how horrible I am, and I know it's true. I wish I could be like you. How do you manage to be nice and sweet?'

Teddy Brown rubbed his nose and scratched his ear. Then he said, 'I was just like you, but I asked Jesus into my heart, and he is changing me, and now I feel happy inside, and peaceful.'

24

'Oh, I wish Jesus would change me. But I'm afraid I'm too nasty.'

'But Jesus can change anyone, if they really want him to.'

'Oh, I do want him to,' said Beauty. 'Would you help me to ask Jesus into my heart so that he can change me?'

So they knelt down and said a prayer together. Beauty said she was sorry for all the times she had been horrid, and asked Jesus to forgive her. Then she said, 'Lord Jesus, please come into my heart and make me like yourself.'

Robby and Teddy Brown went home, but Beauty was ever so much happier. She felt as if a great load had lifted off her, and she wanted to sing. She was much more helpful, and when the other toys got quarrelsome, instead of making things worse, she tried to smooth things over. And every time she was nasty, she asked Jesus to help her, and he made her strong so that she was able to go and say sorry.

One night she had another dream. She was with Teddy Brown in the garden, and the silver aeroplane came down again. They got in, and it went up, up above the clouds. It was as if she was watching herself and Teddy Brown walking round. The people were all smiling at them and saying, 'Look at that fine handsome Teddy Bear, and that beautiful doll. Isn't she lovely!'

When they passed the old gentleman on the bench, he said, 'Oh, little doll, I can see something has happened to you. Why, you're beautiful!'

She heard herself saying to him, 'Thank you— thank you for telling me what I was like. I asked Jesus into my heart, and he has started to change me.'

The old gentleman smiled at her, 'Isn't it wonderful what Jesus can do. You keep his Spirit in your heart, and you will grow more like him.'

Next time Robby and Teddy Brown went to tea with Jemma, she said to Robby, 'D'you know, my doll Beauty is so different—she's changed. She is so sweet and good-tempered and hardly ever has a bad mood. In fact all my toys seem to be getting on better.'

Beauty said to Jemma, 'I haven't told you yet, but last time he was here, Teddy Brown helped me to ask Jesus to start changing me, and I know that is what he is doing.'

Jemma, 'If he can do that to you, I wonder if he could do the same for me.'

Robby said, 'Jesus began a change in me when I asked him into my heart.'

So Jemma asked Jesus into her heart, and she began to grow like him.

And do you know, Jesus can come into your heart too and make you his own child, and you can grow to be more like him.

Suggested Bible Readings

1. Teddy Brown Gets Upset

Proverbs 25:6–7.
Luke 14:7–11.
Philippians 2:5–8.

2. To Podge with Love

Matthew 6:3–4.
Luke 6:32–36.
2 Corinthians 9:7.

3. The Dream

1 Samuel 16:7.
Ezekiel 11:19–20.